HOPSCOTCH
TWISTY TALES

Little Mermaid's Deep Sea Rescue

by Laura North and Dylan Gibson

W
FRANKLIN WATTS
LONDON•SYDNEY

This story is based on the traditional fairy tale,
The Little Mermaid, but with a new twist.
Can you make up your own twist for the story?

Franklin Watts
First published in Great Britain in 2016
by the Watts Publishing Group

Copyright (text) © Laura North 2016
Copyright (illustrations) © Dylan Gibson 2016

The rights of Laura North to be identified as the
author and Dylan Gibson as the illustrator of this Work have been
asserted in accordance with the Copyright, Designs and
Patents Act, 1988.

ISBN 978 1 4451 4785 7 (hbk)
ISBN 978 1 4451 4787 1 (pbk)
ISBN 978 1 4451 4786 4 (library ebook)

Series Editor: Melanie Palmer
Series Advisor: Catherine Glavina
Series Designer: Peter Scoulding
Cover Designer: Cathryn Gilbert

Printed in China

Franklin Watts
An imprint of
Hachette Children's Group
Part of The Watts Publishing Group
Carmelite House
50 Victoria Embankment
London EC4Y 0DZ

An Hachette UK Company
www.hachette.co.uk

www.franklinwatts.co.uk

MIX
Paper from
responsible sources
FSC® C104740
FSC
www.fsc.org

The Little Mermaid was out
swimming with her sister.

"I saw a handsome prince on a ship," swooned her sister. "Boring!" said the Little Mermaid.

"I wish I had legs, so I could go
and meet him," said her sister.
"Why do you want legs?" said
the Little Mermaid. "Tails are
so much better!"

One day, a fishing boat sailed past.
The fishermen lowered their nets.

"Help!" The Little Mermaid's tail was stuck. She was pulled up, up, up until ...

8

THUD! She landed on the hard wooden deck of the boat. She would die if she was out of the water too long.

A fisherman stared at her.

She stared back.

"You're so beautiful," he said.

"And you have a tail!"

"Yes, brainbox," she said.

"Now throw me back in the sea!"

He looked at her in amazement.

"Quickly!" she shouted.

"My name's Hunter. What's yours?" said the young man. "Jasmine," said the mermaid, as she swam away.

"Hunter!" yelled his dad. "You've ruined my net!" All Hunter could think about was the strange woman he'd just met.

Hunter could not wait any longer. He had to find Jasmine. He dived into the sea and began to search.

Suddenly, he saw a shark's fin. "Help!" Hunter cried as the shark opened its jaws wide ...

Jasmine heard him and rushed up.

"Stop! Don't eat him he's a friend."

"OK, Jasmine," said the shark.

"I won't eat him, just this once!"

"What are you doing here?"
Jasmine asked Hunter.
"I was looking for you,"
Hunter replied.

"Oh," she said, secretly pleased.

"Do you want to stay in the water with me?" she said.

"Yes!" said Hunter. "But I can't hold my breath for long."

"I will ask the Sea Wizard to make you a potion," said Jasmine.

In a flash Hunter had a tail.

He could also breathe under water.

Jasmine and Hunter went on lots
of dates. They went to the cinema.
They went for dinner. They even
played Puffa Ball!

Hunter's dad was worried. He searched the seas for his missing son. Finally he found him. "You've got a tail!" he cried.

Hunter's dad was glad his son was alive. He could see how happy he was, even with a tail!

"We'll come back up to see you,
I promise," said Hunter.
And they did, every Sunday
evening.

Puzzle 1

Put these pictures in the correct order.
Which event do you think is most important?
Now try writing the story in your own words!

Puzzle 2

Choose the correct speech bubbles for each character. Can you think of any others? Turn over to find the answers.

Answers

Puzzle 1

The correct order is: 1f, 2c, 3e, 4a, 5d, 6b

Puzzle 2

Jasmine: 3, 4

Hunter: 1, 6

Dad: 2, 5

Look out for more Hopscotch Twisty Tales

The Ninjabread Man
ISBN 978 1 4451 3964 7
The Boy Who Cried Sheep!
ISBN 978 1 4451 4292 0
Thumbelina Thinks Big
ISBN 978 1 4451 4295 1
Move versus the Enormous Turnip
ISBN 978 1 4451 4300 2
Big Pancacke to the Rescue
ISBN 978 1 4451 4303 3
Little Red Hen's Great Escape
ISBN 978 1 4451 4305 7
The Lovely Duckling
ISBN 978 1 4451 1633 4
Hansel and Gretel and the Green Witch
ISBN 978 1 4451 1634 1
The Emperor's New Kit
ISBN 978 1 4451 1635 8

Rapunzel and the Prince of Pop
ISBN 978 1 4451 1636 5
Dick Whittington Gets on his Bike
ISBN 978 1 4451 1637 2
The Pied Piper and the Wrong Song
ISBN 978 1 4451 1638 9
The Princess and the Frozen Peas
ISBN 978 1 4451 0675 5
Snow White Sees the Light
ISBN 978 1 4451 0676 2
The Elves and the Trendy Shoes
ISBN 978 1 4451 0678 6
The Three Frilly Goats Fluff
ISBN 978 1 4451 0677 9

Princess Frog
ISBN 978 1 4451 0679 3
Rumpled Stilton Skin
ISBN 978 1 4451 0680 9
Jack and the Bean Pie
ISBN 978 1 4451 0182 8
Brownilocks and the Three Bowls of Cornflakes
ISBN 978 1 4451 0183 5
Cinderella's Big Foot
ISBN 978 1 4451 0184 2
Little Bad Riding Hood
ISBN 978 1 4451 0185 9
Sleeping Beauty – 100 Years Later
ISBN 978 1 4451 0186 6
The Three Little Pigs & the New Neighbour
ISBN 978 1 4451 0181 1